Dear Parents, Educators, and Guardians,

Thank you for helping your child dive into this book with us. We believe in the power of books to transport readers to other worlds, expand their horizons, and help them discover cultures and experiences that may differ from their own.

We also believe that books should inspire young readers to imagine a diverse world that includes them, a world in which they can see themselves as the heroes of their own stories.

These are our hopes for *all* our readers. So come on. Dive into reading and explore the world with us!

Best wishes,
Your friends at Lee & Low

Follow That Map!

WITHDRAWN

Henry   Lily   Mei   Pablo   Padma

by **Sheri Tan**

illustrated by **Shirley Ng-Benitez**

Lee & Low Books Inc.   New York

To Fernando, Alejandro, and Javier, for making each trip
to Coney Island a great adventure. —S.T.

To the reader: set out on an adventure and discover the gifts
of new communities! —S.N-B.

LEE & LOW BOOKS Inc., 95 Madison Avenue, New York, NY 10016, leeandlow.com
Book design by Maria Mercado
Book production by The Kids at Our House
The illustrations are rendered in watercolor and altered digitally
Manufactured in China by Imago
Printed on paper from responsible sources
(hc) 10 9 8 7 6 5 4 3 2 1
(pb) 10 9 8 7 6 5 4 3 2 1
First Edition

Library of Congress Cataloging-in-Publication Data
Names: Tan, Sheri, author. | Ng-Benitez, Shirley, illustrator.
Title: Follow that map! / by Sheri Tan; illustrated by Shirley Ng-Benitez.
Description: First edition. | New York: Lee & Low Books Inc., [2019] |
   Series: [Dive into reading; 8] | Summary: Pablo invites his friends to go
   with him and his father to Coney Island to celebrate the end of summer,
   using his trusty maps to guide their way by bus and subway train.
Identifiers: LCCN 2018049339 | ISBN 9781620145692 (Hardcover)
   ISBN 9781620145708 (Paperback)
Subjects: | CYAC: Maps—Fiction. | Buses—Fiction. | Subways—Fiction.
   Friendship—Fiction. | Coney Island (New York, N.Y.)—Fiction.
Classification: LCC PZ7.T16125 Fol 2019 | DDC [E]—dc23
LC record available at https://lccn.loc.gov/2018049339

Contents

A Fun Plan

"Summer is almost over," said Lily. "I know a great way to end the summer," said Pablo.

"Let's go to Coney Island!"

"We can ride bumper cars!"
said Padma.
"We can play ring toss!"
said Henry.
"We can play on the beach!"
said Mei.

"That sounds like fun," said Lily.
"But how do we get there?"
"We will use maps," said Pablo.
"Coney Island, here we come!"

At home, Pablo asked his dad,
"Can you please take my friends
and me to Coney Island?"
"Yes," said Pablo's dad.
"I love Coney Island!"

Pablo liked maps.
He liked to find new places.
He also liked to find the best
way to get there.

"We will need to take the bus
and then the subway,"
said Pablo.
"That is the best way to get to
Coney Island," said Pablo's dad.

Maps

Pablo found Coney Island
on the map.
It was near the subway.
But Pablo and his friends lived
near a bus stop.

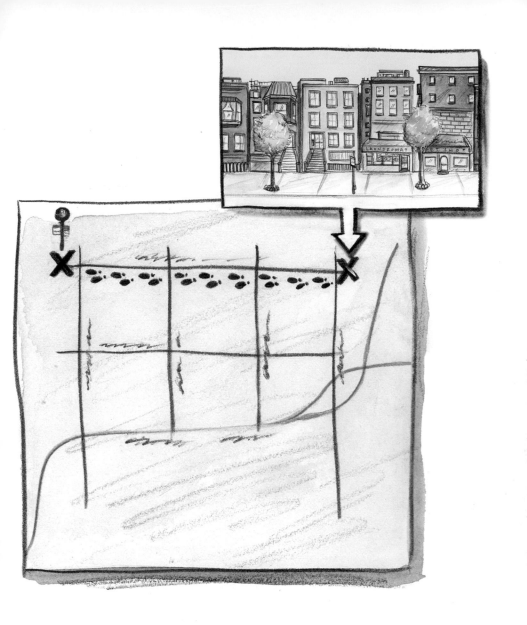

Next he found the best way
to walk from his house to
the bus stop.
They would take the bus to
the subway.

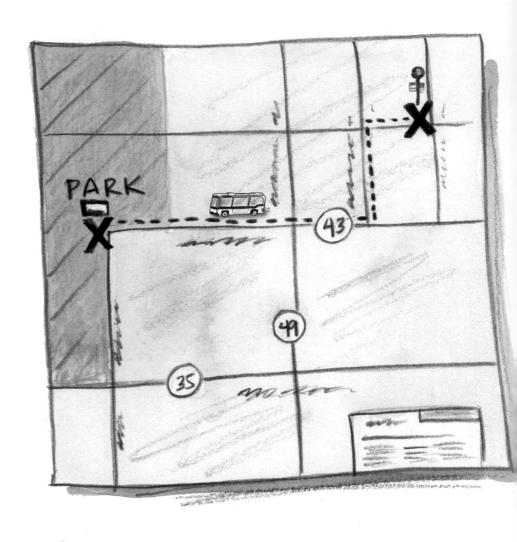

Pablo looked at the streets
the bus would take to get
to the subway station.

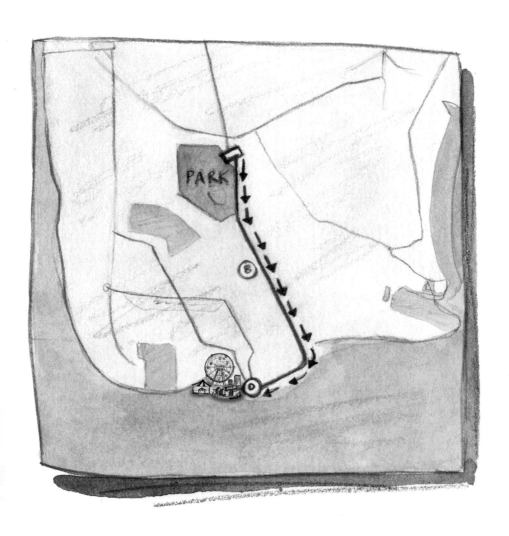

Pablo looked at where the
subway would go to get
to Coney Island.
"We are ready!" said Pablo.

The next day Pablo met his friends.
"I have all the maps we need,"
Pablo told his friends.
"Maps?" Padma and Mei asked.
"Yes," said Pablo.
"It will be fun."

Pablo liked maps.
But would his friends think
it was fun to follow a map?

Soon the bus came.
They got on and paid.
They all sat together.

They saw their neighborhood
from the bus.
They saw the library.
They saw the public garden.

The bus moved slowly.
"Are we there yet?" asked Henry.
"Let me look at my map,"
said Pablo.

"We are close to the subway station," said Pablo.

"How far away?" asked Padma.

"Just three more stops," said Pablo.

Everyone counted the stops.

A woman on crutches
got on the bus.
Henry and Pablo stood up.
"You can sit here,"
they told her.

"Thank you," said the woman.
"You are both very kind."

"The next stop is the subway
station," said Pablo.
"Finally!" said Henry.
Pablo pressed a button.
Soon the bus stopped.

"Thank you!" said Pablo, his friends, and dad to the bus driver.
They got off the bus.

Pablo looked at another map.
"We will take that train,"
said Pablo.
"It is going to Coney Island."

"It looks like *everyone* is going to Coney Island," said Mei.

The train moved quickly.
"Are we almost there?"
asked Lily.

"Let me look at my map,"
said Pablo.
"It looks like we are close
to Coney Island."

They saw the sign for
Coney Island.
"We are here!" said Pablo.

"That was a really long trip,"
said Henry.
"Good thing we had your maps."
"It was fun," said Lily.
"We got to see so much."

"What do we do now?"
asked Padma.
"Let me look at my map,"
said Pablo.
"Why do we need another
map?" asked Mei.
"We are at Coney Island."

"It's a map of all the rides,"
said Pablo.
"Come on, let's go!"

Activity

Can you make a map of your neighborhood?

1. On a piece of paper, draw where you live in the center.

2. Next, draw any shops, parks, friends' houses, and other places nearby that you can remember.

3. With an adult and your map, walk around your neighborhood. What do you need to add or change on your map of the neighborhood?

4. Include street names, bus stops, and bike paths too.

Now you have a map of your neighborhood!

Sheri Tan is a freelance editor who has also written many books for children. She loves public transit in different cities around the world, but the one she's most fond of is the New York City subway system, because it takes her home. Tan lives in Queens, New York, with her husband and their two sons.

Shirley Ng-Benitez loves to draw and write. She creates her art with watercolor, gouache, pencil, and digital techniques. She lives in the San Francisco Bay Area, and is inspired by nature, her family, her pup, and her two kittens.

Read More About Pablo and His Friends!